WIGGLESBOTTOM PRIMARY
PRIMARY
BREAK-TIME BUNNIES

THERE'S
LOADS MORE
MAYHEM IN

WIGGLESBOTTOM PRIMARY

THE TOILET
GHOST

THE SHARK
IN THE POOL

THE MAGIC
HAMSTER

SUPER
DOG

THE
CLASSROOM
CAT

WIGGLESBOTTOM PRIMARY
BREAK-TIME BUNNIES

PAMELA BUTCHART

BECKA MOOR

nosy crow

WELCOME TO
WIGGLESBOTTOM PRIMARY!

MISS RILEY

HANA

LAUREN

JAYDEN

IRFAN

EVIE

MEGAN

MILES

SUSIE

MR HARRIS

ROZ

SUNITA

GAVIN

JOEL

ANNE-MARIE

BOBBY

THEO

First published in 2020 by Nosy Crow Ltd
The Crow's Nest, 14 Baden Place,
Crosby Row, London SE1 1YW

www.nosycrow.com

ISBN: 978 1 78800 123 6

Printed in Spain.

Papers used by Nosy Crow are made
from wood grown in
sustainable forests.

1 3 5 7 9 8 6 4 2

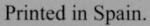

CONTENTS

FOR MICHELLE ORMOND. THANK
YOU FOR EVERYTHING YOU DID
FOR ME AND ALBIE. IT MEANT
THE WORLD TO ME. THIS BOOK
IS FOR YOU AND YOUR BOYS.
LOVE FROM PAMELA AND ALBIE
X X X

FOR J
B. M.

BREAK-TIME BUNNIES

On Monday, as soon as we got to our classroom, Susie Keys pointed out of the window and

GASPED.

So we all ran over to see what the **GASPING** was about and that's when we saw that there were **FOUR** bunnies sitting on the Grassy Bit in the playground. And they were so cute!

Gavin Ross pointed to one of the bunnies and said that it was the **COOLEST** bunny he'd ever **SEEN** because it had a little black patch on one eye and it looked like a pirate.

But then Susie Keys said the pure white one was **OBVIOUSLY** the best because it was making a **NEST**.

So that's when Roz Morgan said that she didn't think bunnies made **NESTS** and Susie crossed her arms and said that they **DEFINITELY DID**. And then Sunita Ram got involved because she **ALWAYS** gets involved when there's an argument.

But then all of a sudden everyone **STOPPED** arguing about the **NEST** because Jayden King squealed a bit and shouted,

"LOOK!"

So we all followed his finger to where he was pointing and **THAT'S** when we saw that there weren't just **FOUR** bunnies on the Grassy Bit any more because there were **TEN**.

That's when everyone started to **PANIC** because we had **NO IDEA** where all the bunnies were coming from and it definitely wasn't **NORMAL**.

Sunita Ram **RAN** to get Miss Riley and when she'd managed to pull her over to the window there were **FIFTEEN BUNNIES** on the Grassy Bit!

Miss Riley got a **REALLY WEIRD** look on her face when she saw the bunnies and said she was going to get Mr Harris, the head teacher, so we knew that this was **SERIOUS**.

But by the time Mr Harris got there, there were **TWENTY BUNNIES**!

That's when Mr Harris said that we all had to go to an **ASSEMBLY**.

And that wasn't **NORMAL** because usually assemblies are on a **FRIDAY**. And **NORMALLY** we get to take our coats and bags off first and hang them on our pegs. But Mr Harris said that there **WASN'T TIME** and that it was an

EMERGENCY ASSEMBLY.

So we all went to the **EMERGENCY ASSEMBLY** with our coats and bags still on and Mr Harris got up on stage and he looked **PANICKED**.

We had **NO IDEA** what was going on or what Mr Harris was going to say or where all the **BUNNIES** were coming from.

And then Mr Harris said, "Break time is officially **CANCELLED** because of the **BUNNIES**."

And everyone

GASPED

Then **LOADS** of people started putting their hands up and asking about the bunnies but Mr Harris said that there **WASN'T TIME** for questions and then he rushed off the stage.

Then when we were on our way back to class, we overheard one of the Year 4s say that the bunnies were obviously

ATTACK BUNNIES

and that they had been **SENT HERE** by another school to take us over!

None of us had any idea what

ATTACK BUNNIES

were but we knew that they obviously weren't good and that we were probably all in **SERIOUS DANGER**.

When we got back to class Miss Riley tried to take our minds off the **BREAK-TIME BUNNIES** by closing the blinds so we couldn't see them. But none of us could concentrate because every two minutes Miss Riley would lean over her desk and peek through the blinds to check how many bunnies there were now.

Jayden King said that there were probably **HUNDREDS** of bunnies out there. But Irfan Baxter shook his head and said that there were probably **THOUSANDS** and maybe even **MILLIONS**, and that they were getting ready to **ATTACK**.

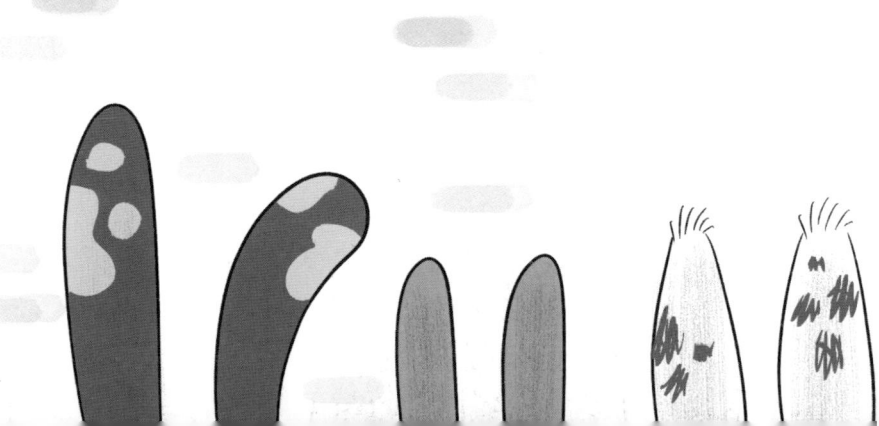

And that's when Susie Keys got up and started putting her coat on and said that she was going home, because that's what she always does when she gets scared. And then she ran out of the classroom before anyone could stop her.

So Miss Riley ran after her, and so did we because we didn't want the **ATTACK BUNNIES** to get her.

But then when we were all running along the corridor Susie started running **BACK** towards us and she looked like she'd seen a **GHOST**.

And **THAT'S** when we all looked out the corridor window and saw Mr Harris was standing in the **MIDDLE** of the Grassy Bit and he was **COMPLETELY SURROUNDED BY BUNNIES**! And he had a really weird smile on his face.

17

We all got such a fright that we ran
SCREAMING back to the classroom.
Then Sunita Ram said that we needed to
get up on top of our desks, so that if the
ATTACK BUNNIES made their way
into the school and along the corridor they
wouldn't be able to get us because bunnies
can't **JUMP**.

So we all stood on top of the desks even though Miss Riley was telling us not to and then **ONE SECOND LATER** Mr Harris walked into our classroom and we all **GASPED** because we had **NO IDEA** how he'd got all the way up here so fast because we'd just seen him outside on the Grassy Bit!

And that's when Irfan cried, **"OH NO!"** And he jumped down from his desk and **RAN** over to the story-time carpet and gave us a **SIGNAL** that we should all follow him, so we did.

And Miss Riley didn'l even say a **WORD** to us because she was too busy listening to whatever Mr Harris was saying.

So we all sat down and Sunita asked Irfan if we needed to take a deep breath before he said whatever he was going to say and he nodded **LOADS** so we did.

And that's when Irfan said that he knew **EXACTLY** what was going on with the bunnies and that they were **CLONING THEMSELVES** which meant that they were making loads and loads of **COPIES** of themselves and that they probably weren't going to stop until they had a **FULL BUNNY ARMY**.

And then Megan McNally **GASPED** and said, "**MR HARRIS**! That's how he got here so quickly!"

And Irfan nodded and said, "Yes." And then he pointed over to Mr Harris and said, "That's not the real Mr Harris. That's a **CLONE**. I think they must have needed a **HUMAN** so they chose him and made him their **LEADER**."

And we all nodded because Mr Harris is the head teacher so that made sense. Then Irfan said that there were probably **LOADS** of Mr Harrises by now and we all started **SCREAMING** because it was **HORRIBLE** to imagine loads of Mr Harrises running around the school telling everyone off because **NO ONE** wants **HUNDREDS** of **HEAD TEACHERS** in their school!

And that's when Mr Harris came over and asked us what we were all screaming about and Susie Keys shouted, **"STAY AWAY, BREAK-TIME BUNNY LEADER!"**

Mr Harris looked really confused so we told him we knew about the **CLONING**.

And that's when Mr Harris said he wasn't a clone and that he'd cancelled **BREAK TIME** because he was worried we would all get **OBSESSED** with the bunnies if we were allowed outside to see them because they were **SUPER-CUTE**.

Then he said that someone was on their way to **COLLECT** all the bunnies because they'd escaped from a local breeding centre and that they were loving the long grass in the Grassy Bit. And then he looked a bit **SAD** and we knew it was because he thought the bunnies were really cute and he missed them **MISSED THEM**.

But then at the end of the day when we were going home we saw Mr Harris getting into his car, which was parked in the car park. And that's when Susie Keys **GASPED** and said, "Look at his bag!"

And we saw that there was a bunny's head poking out of his bag! And we heard Mr Harris say, "There, there, Flopsy, you're going to love your new home. I've got **LOADS** of carrots for you."

And Sunita Ram gasped and said that Mr Harris must still be the leader of the **ATTACK BUNNIES** and that he was going to start a new **BUNNY ARMY**!
And we all **RAN**!

29

THE SPECIAL GUEST

One day, Miss Riley (that's our teacher) said that a **SPECIAL GUEST** would be coming to our class.

And then she got a **NERVOUS LOOK** on her face and said, "Our special guest might ask you questions about me."

We all looked at each other because we didn't know who this

SPECIAL GUEST

was or why they would ask **US** questions about Miss Riley when they could just ask her themselves.

That's when Joel Jack pointed at Miss Riley and did a **WEIRD WINKING THING** and said, **"GOTCHA."**

Bul Miss Riley didn't notice because she was too busy tidying her desk and taking all the empty crisp packets out of her drawers and putting them in the bin.

That's when Joel Jack said that the **SPECIAL GUEST** was **OBVIOUSLY** the man from the TV who does all the

TALENT SHOWS

and that he must be coming here so he could find out if Miss Riley was **GOOD ENOUGH** to be on a big TV talent show.

Lauren Carr said, "Like an audition?" And Joel Jack nodded loads.

EVERYONE started to get really excited about the

TALENT MAN

coming to our classroom and Jayden King
even did a bit of a

DANCE THING

and said that he was going to audition,
too.

Sunita Ram said that when the **SPECIAL GUEST** arrived we all needed to tell them how **TALENTED** Miss Riley was so that she got to go on TV.

But none of us knew what Miss Riley's **TALENT** was.

Lauren Carr said that Miss Riley's talent might be writing on the **WHITEBOARD** really **NEATLY**.

But Joel Jack said that that was **BORING** and that you didn't get on TV just because you could write **NEATLY** and that Miss Riley must have a **HIDDEN TALENT** that we didn't know about.

Then all of a sudden there was a knock at the door and a man with no hair and loads of **FOLDERS** came in.

The man didn't look anything **LIKE** the man from TV but then Joel Jack said that people from TV always look different in **REAL LIFE** and that one time his gran saw **THE QUEEN** in Morrisons and that it had taken her **AGES** to figure out who it was because she looked so different in real life, next to the eggs.

We all **STARED** at the man. But he didn't even **LOOK** at us **OR** at Miss Riley.

He just walked in and took a seat at the back of the classroom and opened up one of his folders. Then Joel said, "This is it, people!" And we all nodded because Miss Riley's **AUDITION** had obviously started.

We all crossed our fingers and **STARED** at Miss Riley because we couldn't **WAIT** to see what her **HIDDEN TALENT** was.

But then Miss Riley started speaking in a bit of a weird voice and twirling her hands **ALL OVER** the place when she was talking.

Joel Jack whispered that he thought Miss Riley's **HIDDEN TALENT** must be

HAND DANCING.

And that made sense because she definitely wasn't using her hands like she normally did, and I had never actually **SEEN** someone twirl their hands around as much as Miss Riley was doing.

Miss Riley was obviously really nervous about her scary **HAND-DANCING AUDITION** because she kept dropping the whiteboard markers when she was trying to write on the board and getting our names mixed up and we kept having to help by picking up the pens and telling her our real names, over and over again.

Miss Riley's audition obviously wasn't going very well and as soon as the bell went our **SPECIAL GUEST** rushed out and Miss Riley flopped on to her chair and put her head down on the desk.

That's when Joel Jack said that it was **"ALL OVER"** and that Miss Riley had failed her audition because **PROFESSIONAL HAND DANCERS** don't drop the board markers ten times during their act.

But then Jayden King said that it wasn't over until it was **OVER** and then he ran out of the classroom.

We had **NO IDEA** what Jayden was up to so Sunita shouted, **"FOLLOW HIM!"** And we did. And when we found him he was standing outside the **STAFF ROOM**.

STAFF ONLY

Jayden said that it was **UP TO US** to convince the talent man to give Miss Riley a **SECOND AUDITION**.

So we knocked on the staff-room door and said that we needed to speak to the **TALENT MAN**, please. But Mr Harris didn't know who we were talking about.

So we peeked through the door and pointed and Mr Harris got a **WEIRD LOOK** on his face and he said, "Why do you need to speak to Mr Powell?"

So we told Mr Harris that we wanted to tell Mr Powell how **TALENTED** Miss Riley was and Mr Harris started smiling **LOADS** and saying that that was a **GREAT IDEA** and then he pushed us towards where Mr Powell was sitting by himself eating a sandwich.

So that's when we started saying **LOADS** of stuff about Miss Riley's **HANDS**. Like how **LONG** her fingernails were and how well she could usually **HOLD A PEN**

and how **EXCELLENT** she was at **WAVING**.

Then Sunita started talking about all the different colours of nail polish Miss Riley had and that's when Mr Harris started pushing us back towards the door again and saying that it was time for us to get to class even though the bell hadn't gone yet.

But Jayden King folded his arms and said that we weren't going **ANYWHERE** until Mr Powell gave Miss Riley a **SECOND CHANCE** because she was probably the most **TALENTED TEACHER** in the whole school and maybe even the **WORLD**.

Everyone **STARED** at Mr Powell to see what he would say, especially Mr Harris.

Then Mr Powell stood up and brushed the sandwich crumbs off his little waistcoat and said, "OK."

So we all **RACED** along to the classroom to warn Miss Riley about her **SECOND AUDITION** so she could do some **FINGER EXERCISES** to get her hands ready before Mr Powell arrived.

Miss Riley still had her head on the desk when we got there but she lifted it up **STRAIGHTAWAY** when we told her Mr Powell was on his way.

As soon as Mr Powell was sat at the back of the classroom again with all his folders Miss Riley told us that it was time to get back to our **SHAKESPEARE PROJECT** and then she brought out loads of **COSTUMES**

and we all got to wear them and pretend we were the characters in the **PLAY** and it was **SO GOOD** that we completely forgot about Mr Powell and Miss Riley's **HAND-DANCING AUDITION.**

When the bell for lunch rang Mr Powell stood up and walked over to Miss Riley and shook her hand and said, **"WELL DONE. THAT WAS EXCELLENT!"**

And we all cheered because we knew that Miss Riley had passed her audition and that she was going to be **ON TV!**

As soon as Mr Powell left, Mr Harris came rushing in and Miss Riley gave him a **THUMBS UP**.

Then Joel Jack asked what day Miss Riley was going to be on TV doing her **HAND DANCING** because he wanted to **RECORD IT** and Miss Riley got a weird look on her face and said, "My *what*?"

And that's when we found out that Miss Riley **WASN'T** a professional **HAND DANCER** and that she definitely **WASN'T** going to be on TV and that she had only been doing the **WEIRD HAND TWIRLING** because she was **NERVOUS**.

Mr Harris said that Mr Powell was a **SCHOOL INSPECTOR** and that he had come to **EVALUATE** our school and watch Miss Riley teach.

And Sunita said, "So it **WAS** an audition then?"

And Mr Harris smiled and said, "Yes, I suppose it was. An audition for the most talented teacher ... and Miss Riley won!"

So we all cheered again and Miss Riley laughed and said, "Thank you. Thank you." And then she started twirling her hands **ALL OVER** the place to make us laugh and it was **HILARIOUS**.

And that's when we all knew that Jayden King was right and that Miss Riley **WAS** the best teacher in the world!

THE BEWITCHED VIOLIN

One day, Miss Riley asked us if there was anyone who would like to learn to play the violin and we **ALL** put our hands up.

But then Miss Riley introduced us to **MISS STEIN** and she was **TALL** and wore **REALLY DARK CLOTHES** and she looked a bit **SPOOKY**.

Miss Stein said that if we wanted to learn to play the violin **PROPERLY** we would have to

WORK HARD

and practise

EVERY DAY.

And that's when everyone put their hands down because it didn't sound like that much fun any more and also because Miss Stein had a bit of a scary voice.

But I kept my hand up because I really wanted to learn how to play a **MUSICAL INSTRUMENT**.

Miss Stein **STARED** at me for ages and then she said, "Come with me, Hana."

And that's when I realised that I was the only one with my hand up and that I was going to be the only one in the **WHOLE CLASS** who was going to learn the **VIOLIN** with **SPOOKY MISS STEIN**.

I was just about to say that I didn't want to do it any more but then Anne-Marie Moor put her hand up and said, "I've changed my mind! I want to come."

And then Bobby Henderson said, "Me too!"

Miss Stein nodded her head and said, "Very well. Follow me."

So we all followed Miss Stein along the corridor and down the stairs. And we actually had to **RUN** a bit to keep up with her because she was walking **REALLY QUICKLY** and her long, dark cardigan was floating behind her and it looked a bit like a **SPOOKY CAPE**.

73

When we got to the bottom floor, Miss Stein opened a door that we didn't even know **EXISTED** and disappeared inside.

That's when Anne-Marie Moor said that she was **ONE HUNDRED PER CENT** sure that the door hadn't been there this

morning and Bobby Henderson
said that he wasn't going inside
and that the only reason he'd put his
hand back up was because he wanted to
get out of class for a while.

But then we heard **MUSIC** coming from

the room so we peeked inside and that's when we saw that it was **FULL** of old, dusty instruments and boxes and things covered with **SHEETS**.

And that Miss Stein was playing the violin.
We all watched and listened as Miss Stein
played a **REALLY LONG** and **SHAKY**
note on the violin.

And then she stood up and handed us each a violin case and showed us how to **OPEN** the case and how to **HOLD** the violin properly and how to rub the little red **ROSIN** on the bow to make the bow work better.

And then she said, "OK. Put your fingers here, like this and try to play this note. Anne-Marie, you can go first."

Anne-Marie pulled her bow across the violin strings and it made a loud, screeching sound and it didn't sound **ANYTHING** like the nice sound Miss Stein had made.

Then Miss Stein pointed her bow at me and I tried to play the note but it sounded even **WORSE** than Anne-Marie's had. So I said sorry to everyone because the sound had been so **LOUD** and so **SCREECHY** that they'd all covered their ears, even Miss Stein.

But Miss Stein said that there was **NO**

NEED to apologise and that we were **BEGINNERS** and that **EVERYONE** sounded bad when they first started and that it would take **YEARS** for us to learn to play as well as she could.

But **JUST** as Miss Stein was finishing her sentence Bobby started playing the long note and it sounded all **SHAKY** and **PROFESSIONAL** and it sounded even **BETTER** than when Miss Stein had played it!

Miss Stein's eyes went **WIDE** and we all **GASPED** because we had **NO IDEA** Bobby could play the violin better than an actual **VIOLIN TEACHER**.

Miss Stein asked Bobby how long he'd been playing the violin for and he said, "Um. One minute?"

That's when Miss Stein got a **REALLY WEIRD** look on her face and said, **"LESSON OVER! BACK TO CLASS!"** And then she ran out the door ahead of us and along the corridor.

So we all went back to class and told everyone about Bobby being able to play the violin even though he'd never even **TOUCHED ONE** before.

Bobby said that he had **NO IDEA** how he'd been able to play the violin. And that's when Anne-Marie Moor said that she knew **EXACTLY** how and that Bobby's violin was

BEWITCHED

and that Miss Stein was the one who had **BEWITCHED** it because she was a bewitching **WITCH**. Anne-Marie said that she had **SUSPECTED** that Miss Stein was a **WITCH** and that that was why she'd changed her mind and put her hand back up because she wanted to keep a

CLOSE EYE on her.

Everyone

GASPED.

And we knew that Anne-Marie was right because we'd all seen Miss Stein's **LONG BLACK DRESS** and **CARDIGAN CAPE**.

Then at lunchtime, Bobby said that he was feeling a bit **WEIRD** and that his **FINGERTIPS** were **TINGLING** and Anne-Marie **GASPED** and said that meant

Miss Stein was **CLOSE** and that she was probably casting a **SPELL** on his fingers so that he could play the violin **EVEN BETTER** than before!

Then all of a sudden Miss Stein appeared at our table and we all **SCREAMED** because she had appeared out of **THIN AIR**.

Miss Stein **STARED** at Bobby. And then she said, "Come with me."

And Bobby got up and went with Miss Stein really quickly before we could do anything to stop him.

As soon as they were gone Anne-Marie said, "Mr Harris. **NOW!**" and then she ran. So we all ran after her because we knew that she was **RIGHT** and that we had to tell the head teacher about Miss Stein being a

BEWITCHING WITCH

before she flew away with Bobby and forced him to play the violin to her all day, every day, in her faraway witchy **CASTLE**.

But when we got to Mr Harris's office, Bobby and Miss Stein were there and Bobby had his **COAT AND BAG ON** even though it wasn't home time yet. And Miss

Stein was staring at Mr Harris and he was
NODDING LOADS.

That's when Anne-Marie shouted, "**STOP BEWITCHING MR HARRIS!** Bobby's not going **ANYWHERE** with you!"

Miss Stein got such a shock that she dropped her violin on the ground and when she saw that it had broken she did a loud **WITCH SCREAM**.

Anne-Marie shouted, "COVER YOUR EARS OR YOU'LL TURN TO STONE!"

So we all covered our ears and screamed at the **TOP OF OUR LUNGS** because we were **TERRIFIED**.

EVERYONE was screaming and Mr Harris had to **BLOW HIS WHISTLE** to get us to stop. And when we stopped screaming we saw that Miss Stein was sitting on the floor trying to fix her violin.

Mr Harris told us all to **EXPLAIN OURSELVES**. So we did. We explained about **BOBBY** and the **VIOLIN** and the **STARING** and the **TINGLING FINGERS** and all the **BEWITCHING**.

And that's when Miss Stein stopped looking so upset and smiled a bit. And then she said that she **WASN'T** a witch but that she wished she **WAS** because then she could use her **POWERS** to fix her violin.

And when she said that we all felt **TERRIBLE**.

Miss Stein said that Bobby was so good at the violin because he was a **NATURAL** and maybe even a **MUSICAL GENIUS** and that she'd just been telling Mr Harris all about Bobby and his **TALENT** and how she was going to give Bobby **LESSONS** for **FREE**.

And then Anne-Marie asked if Bobby was

moving schools to go to a violin school now that he was a **MUSICAL GENIUS** and was that why he had his coat and bag on. But Bobby said no and that he just had a dentist appointment.

But then Bobby said that his fingers were tingling again and Miss Stein asked to see them and said, "I think you've been pressing on the strings too hard. Rest them and they'll feel better in a few hours. I'll see you tomorrow before lunch for your lesson."

And then she left.

SO we all made sure Bobby **RESTED HIS FINGERS** that day and Anne-Marie

even did all his **WRITING** for him in class.

But then at home time when we were walking out of the school Anne-Marie **GASPED** and said that she didn't remember seeing the **SECRET DOOR** and **NONE** of us could remember seeing it either and we couldn't even go back in to check because our mums and dads were already waiting for us.

And that's when Anne-Marie said, "You don't think Miss Stein maybe **IS** a witch after all, do you?"

And we all

GASPED.